For my niece Alexandra, fashionista and channeler
of the pirate spirit of adventure.
—N. R. D.

For my son, Quinn. I wish you a life filled with bold
adventures and colorful friendships.
—A. B.

BEACH LANE BOOKS · An imprint of Simon & Schuster Children's Publishing Division · 1230 Avenue of the Americas, New York, New York 10020
Text copyright © 2018 by Nancy Raines Day · Illustrations copyright © 2018 by Allison Black
All rights reserved, including the right of reproduction in whole or in part in any form. · BEACH LANE BOOKS is a trademark of Simon & Schuster, Inc.
For information about special discounts for bulk purchases, please contact Simon & Schuster Special Sales at 1-866-506-1949 or business@simonandschuster.com.
The Simon & Schuster Speakers Bureau can bring authors to your live event. For more information or to book an event, contact the Simon & Schuster Speakers Bureau at
1-866-248-3049 or visit our website at www.simonspeakers.com.
Book design by Lauren Rille · The text for this book was set in Brandon Grotesque. · The illustrations for this book were rendered in Adobe Photoshop.
Manufactured in China · 0718 SCP · First Edition · 10 9 8 7 6 5 4 3 2 1
Library of Congress Cataloging-in-Publication Data
Names: Day, Nancy Raines, author. | Black, Allison, illustrator.
Title: Pirate Jack gets dressed / Nancy Raines Day ; illustrated by Allison Black.
Description: First edition. | New York : Beach Lane Books, [2018]
Summary: Through illustrations and simple, rhyming text a pirate invites the reader to help as he selects his very colorful outfit.
Identifiers: LCCN 2017038886 | ISBN 9781481476645 (hardcover : alk. paper) | ISBN 9781481476652 (eBook)
Subjects: | CYAC: Stories in rhyme. | Pirates—Fiction. | Clothing and dress—Fiction. | Color—Fiction.
Classification: LCC PZ8.3.D3334 Pir 2017 | DDC [E]—dc23 LC record available at https://lccn.loc.gov/2017038886

PIRATE ☠ JACK
GETS DRESSED

written by
Nancy Raines Day

illustrated by
Allison Black

BEACH LANE BOOKS
New York · London · Toronto
Sydney · New Delhi

AHOY THERE,

Jack's me name.
I'm a pirate—
that's me game.

At crack o' dawn, I stretch and yawn,
and scratch me itchy, GRAY long johns.

I pull me eye patch from me sack.
A pirate has t' wear some **BLACK**.

Who's in me glass? Aye, aye, that's me.
I sport **GOLD** earrings when at sea.

I need a hand for getting dressed—
me **SILVER** hook, ye might've guessed.

I pull on britches, sunny YELLOW.
Have ye ever spied a finer fellow?

Without me shirt I'd be dressed wrong,
although it won't stay WHITE for long.

Now what's the next thing I should do?
I'll cover it with vest o' **BLUE**.

Today I'll wear a sash that's RED
and scarf that's ORANGE upon me head.

What else? Egads, me toes be cold!
Thick socks o' **PINK** are warm, I'm told.

A boot that's **BROWN** slides on one leg
and on the other goes a peg.

It's windy out! I need a coat.
Me **PURPLE** one's the best afloat.

What color be I missin', mate?
Come, tell me quick—I can't be late.

Oh, aye! It's GREEN. I've just the thing.
Jump here, Polly, from yer swing.

Now, with all colors, right on cue . . .

'tis time t' join me motley crew!